Poppy & Ella

3 stories about 2 friends

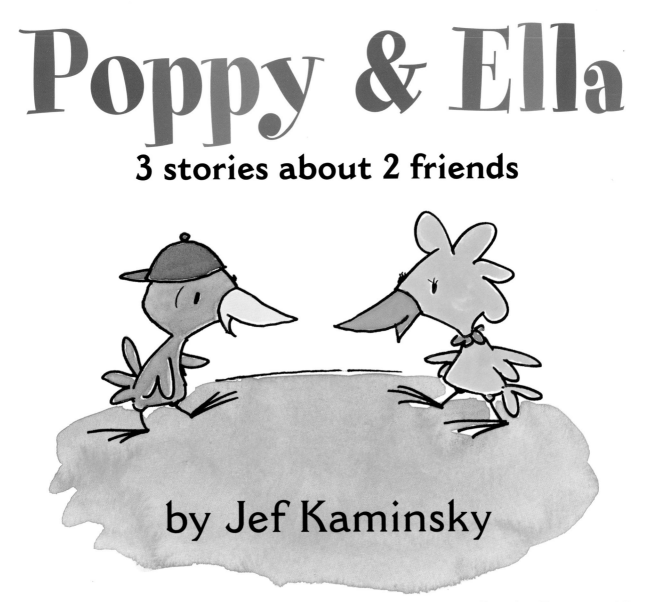

by Jef Kaminsky

Hyperion Books for Children
New York

Library of Congress Cataloging-in-Publication Data
Kaminsky, Jef.
Poppy and Ella: 3 stories about 2 friends/Jef Kaminsky.—1st ed.
p.   cm.
Summary: Two best friends, Poppy and Ella, enjoy lunch,
a day at the beach, and a power outage together.
ISBN 0-7868-0511-0.—ISBN 0-7868-2447-6 (lib. bdg.)
[1. Best friends—Fiction. 2. Birds—Fiction.] I. Title.
PZ7.K12683Po 2000
[E]—dc21   99-28505

Visit www.hyperionchildrensbooks.com, a part of the GO Network

For my own Poppy,
with love and a pot of Bozo beans

"Ruffled Feathers"

One fine morning, Ella and Poppy bumped into each other.

"Poppy, I'm so happy to see you! Why don't you come on over later for some of my excellent Spaghetti alla Ella?"

"Yum!" said Poppy. "I'll see you this afternoon."

Back at home, Poppy ran a comb over his bald head.
"I can't go over to Ella's looking like this!"

So he got out some paper, scissors, and tape.

Poppy began to cut out feathers.
Lots and lots of them!

He taped feathers all over himself.
"Looking good, feeling good."

Poppy zoomed over to Ella's.

"Hello, Poppy. Come on in.
You look . . . um, well, why don't we
just sit down and eat?"

When Poppy leaned forward to take a sip of juice,
he felt some feathers fall off.
"Could you please pass the pepper?" said Ella.
When Poppy reached for the pepper, a whole
bunch more feathers came off.
And then . . .

"ACHOO!"

Ella accidentally giggled.

Poppy split.

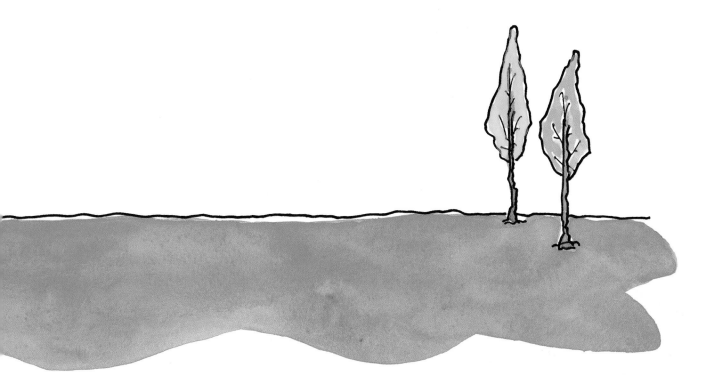

That Poppy can be such a goober at times!
thought Ella as she gathered up the paper
feathers . . .

. . . and took off for Poppy's house.

"Give me a hug, you goober," said Ella, "and I'll teach you a good game."

"To Beach His Own"

Poppy and Ella were spending Saturday at the seashore.
"Where do you want to sit?" asked Ella.

"I like it in the shade," said Poppy.

"No way," said Ella. "I came to the beach to catch some rays, not a cold."

So Ella went to sit in the sunny sun, and Poppy set out his towel in the shady shade.

Poppy kept his beak in his book.

Ella took a catnap.

After a while, Ella woke up. "Hey, shady-bird, let's go swimming!"
"But I just got to a good part in my book," said Poppy.

"Well, Poppy, I'm going swimming right this instant!"

"Hey, Ella, you're getting out already? I'm just going in!"

"Well, now I'm all dry," said Ella.

Poppy and Ella just weren't clicking.

When Ella was flying her kite, Poppy wanted to play ball.

And when Poppy was stacking rocks, Ella was making a castle.

Finally, Ella snapped.

"Poppy! You never want to do what I want to do!"

"Um, Ella?"

"What?"

"If I felt like eating ice cream, would you feel like eating ice cream, too?" asked Poppy.

"Well," said Ella. "Okay."

"Good afternoon," said the ice cream dog. "What flavor would you like?"

"Mint chocolate chip!" said Poppy and Ella together.

"Darkness Falls"

Ella had a secret. A dark secret.
No one, not even Poppy, knew that she was afraid
of the dark.

Ella wasn't getting much sleep.

One evening, Ella was over at Poppy's house
watching TV.
Everything was going great until . . .

...the electricity went off!

"Poppy . . . ? Wh-where are you, Poppy?"

"It's okay, Ella, I'm here. What's wrong?"

"I . . . I didn't tell you before, b-but I'm kind of afraid of the dark," said Ella.

"You? Really?"

"W-well, it's not so much the dark as it is the things you can't see in it."

"Like what?" asked Poppy.

"Oh, the usual—ghosts, witches, house cats . . . mostly house cats."

"Ella, wait right here. Everything's going to be just
fine. I'll be back in a flash!"
Poppy took a little box and went outside.

Ella tried really hard to be brave, but the dark was,
well, *very* dark.

But before she knew it, Poppy came back inside.
"Ella, as soon as you feel scared, take off the lid,
okay?"
"How about—now!" said Ella.

"Fireflies!" said Ella. "Poppy, this is the best dark I've ever seen!"

And after that evening, Ella wasn't afraid of the
dark anymore.
Mostly.